To CHRISTIAN ALEXANDER!

The Kuekumber Kids™ meet

THE MONSTER OF MANNERS

2003

Meet The Kuekumber Kids . . .

This is Kirky Kuekumber.

He'll be six soon.

When he sees an adventure

He's out the door...zoom!

This is Katie Kuekumber

Who is now age four.

She asks lots of questions.

And then she asks more!

This is Krumby,
The Kuekumber kids' dog.
He's a really great pooch
But he eats like a hog.

This is Kirky's Best
Friend, Lance,
Who likes to wear
Colorful pants.

The Kuekumber Kids Meet The Monster of Manners

Action Publishing
PO Box 391,
Glendale, CA 91209

Book and cover design by Yumi Oshima

ISBN: 1-888045-07-8
First Edition
1 2 3 4 5 6 7 8 9 10
Printed in Hong Kong

The Kuekumber Kids™ meet THE MONSTER OF MANNERS

Written and Illustrated by
Scott E. Sutton

There's a party at the Kuekumber's. Why, you say?
'Cause today is Katie Kuekumber's birthday.
But Katie is mad, and as you might guess,
Her birthday party has become a big mess.

Kids are throwing her cake all over the place.

A piece just hit Katie right in the face.

There's ice cream and candy all over the floor

And Katie's poor mom can't take any more.

Katie Kuekumber was about to yell

When she heard "ding, dong" from the front door bell.

Kirky opened the door and to their surprise

Stood a very strange monster of a very large size.

He had skin that was blue, he had hair that was yellow

And he wasn't messy, but a nicely dressed fellow.

He wore a neat suit with a bow tie, too.

He even smelled good, not like an old shoe.

"YIKES!" yelled Katie. "First kids throw my cake.
Now a MONSTER shows up. Oh, what a mistake!"
"Do not fear," said the monster. "I will not hurt you.
This party's a mess, but I know what to do."

"Allow me," said the monster, "to tell you my name.

I'm the Monster of Manners and it is my aim

To save your party. I know why it's a mess.

Because no one has learned their manners, I'd guess."

"Manners? Manners? What are manners?" asked Lance,
Who was wiping some cake off his colorful pants.
"Manners," said the monster, "show you how to treat others,
Like people and parents, your sisters and brothers."

"Now, to help me teach these manners to you
Are the Manners Monsters, Bubby and Shmoo."
"Greetings to you!" the monsters did holler.
They were monsters all right, but quite a bit smaller.

"Fix my party?" asked Katie. "Okay, go ahead."

"No problem. Call me Manny," the big monster said.

"Now the first bunch of manners are how to be clean,

'Cause this is the biggest mess I've ever seen!"

"Okay, kids," said Manny, "we'll start with the floor.

We'll clean this place up 'til the mess is no more."

So they cleaned up the cake and candy, too,

And the ice cream and presents until they were through.

When cleaning the mess up was finally done,
Manny said, "Wash your hands and face everyone."
"But why wash up?" asked Kirky. "How come?
We're gonna get dirty again, that's dumb!"

"Some people," said Manny, "may say 'don't be picky!
You can smell bad, stay dirty and gooey and icky.'
But there is a secret you really must know.
When things stay dirty GERMS can grow."

"Germs? What are germs? " Katie asked quickly.

"Tiny little critters that can make you quite sickly.

They're so small you can't see them," Manny did say.

"Where there's dirt and bad smells they're not far away."

"Wash your hands and face after you play,

Take a bath or shower every day.

Cover your mouth when you cough or you sneeze

Or you'll spray germs on people, so don't do that, please!"

"When you sneeze or have stuff stuck in your nose
Use a tissue to clean it, not your fingers or clothes.
Flush the toilet, too, wash your hands when you're through,
'Cause there's germs in the toilet and it stinks! PU!"

"YIKES!" said Kirky. "That's why you keep clean,

Because of those germs that can't be seen."

"Right," said the monster. "But wait, there's more!

When you leave things a mess on the table or floor"

"Like clothes or food, your toys and all,
People can trip on them, slip and fall.
If your room is a mess," Manny told everyone,
"You can't find anything or get anything done!"

"You look for some crayons. Oh, where could they be?

But to find them in that mess takes a day, maybe three!

It's okay to work, play and have fun

But clean up and pick up your stuff when you're done."

"Now, line up for cake, kids," Manny did say.

"I'll teach you to get things done the right way."

Kids were pushing and yelling for cake and ice cream.

"PLEASE BE QUIET!" Monster Bubby did scream.

The kids became quiet with a look of surprise.

Bubby's voice was so loud for the monster's small size!

"If everyone interrupts when someone is talking,

You can't hear a thing. It's like parrots squawking!"

"Here are some manners you've got to learn.

You can't ALL go at once, you must each wait your turn.

If you all go at once you will smoosh everyone.

Then no one gets nothin' and nothin' gets done!"

"You say PLEASE if you want something done, it's true.
Like 'Please may I have cake and ice cream, too?'
And when someone gives or does something for you
Always say THANK YOU to them when they're through."

The kids and the monsters each got some cake,

Saying PLEASE and THANK YOU without a mistake.

"Close your mouth and don't talk whenever you chew,

Or the food will fall out and that's gross!" said Shmoo.

"What about burping?" asked Kirky Kuekumber.

"Your burps," laughed Katie, "are loud like thunder."

"Cover your mouth when you burp," Bubby said,

"Don't make it so loud. Say EXCUSE ME instead."

"Here's a manner," said Manny, "that's helpful to know,
You'll need EXCUSE ME wherever you go.
To get through a crowd or cross through a line,
Say EXCUSE ME first, you should get through just fine.

"If you meet your friends or someone new,
Smile and say 'Hello'," said Shmoo.
"Then, when you leave, you always should say
Good-bye to them before walking away."

When the kids and the monsters ate and were done
They went outside to play games and have fun.
They played soccer, jump rope and hide-and-seek, too.
But the monsters saw there was more work to do.

Some kids playing ball started yelling and fighting.

They were using bad words, even hitting and biting!

Some girls had taken one of Katie's new toys

And poor Krumby's tail was being pulled by some boys.

Krumby was growling, Katie started to cry.
It was time to give some new manners a try.
So Manny the Monster, with Bubby and Shmoo
Stepped in to show the kids what to do.

The Monster of Manners said, "Listen here, boys.
Don't hurt that poor dog, he's not one of your toys.
How would you like someone to do that to you?
Be nice to animals, they'll be nice to you, too."

"Now, girls," said Manny, "taking things isn't fair.
If you ask Katie nicely, maybe she'll share."
"Don't take others' things without asking," said Shmoo.
Ask first and say PLEASE. It's the right thing to do."

Manny the Monster told the boys playing ball,

"These bad words and hitting are no good at all!"

"Don't hit or hurt people," said Bubby and Shmoo,

"'Cause you wouldn't want them to hit or hurt you."

"If you hurt people's feelings, call 'em names that are bad,
You will lose them as friends and then you'll be sad.
If you want people to be nice to you
You've got to try to be nice to them, too."

"If someone gets hurt, like falls to the ground,
Don't laugh or make fun, don't just stand around.
Make sure they're all right. If they're not okay,
Then go get some help for them right away."

"All right," said Manny, "let's go back through
The manners we monsters have been teaching you:
Keep your body clean, flush the toilet too, please.
Cover your mouth when you cough or you sneeze."

"Use a tissue," said Katie, "to clean your nose.

Pick up and put away your toys and your clothes."

"Close your mouth when you chew your food," Bubby said,

"And don't interrupt, say EXCUSE ME instead."

"Don't cut in," said Lance, "wait your turn.

And PLEASE and THANK YOU are words you must learn."

"Don't take things without asking. Try to share, too.

Don't call people bad names or hit them," said Shmoo.

"Don't hurt your pets, like your dogs, cats or birds,"
Said Kirky Kuekumber. "And don't use bad words."
"Well done!" said Manny. "But before we go.
There's a reason for manners that you need to know."

"All people are different, not just different clothes,
Their bodies different colors, a big or small nose.
Some may be thin, and some may be tubby,
But they're people like you are," said Monster Bubby.

"If you want others to be nice to you,

Try to use manners and be nice to them, too."

"Good-bye!" said Manny, Bubby and Shmoo.

"You've learned your manners, you know what to do."

"Thanks for saving my party," happy Katie did say.

"You're welcome!" said the monsters and went on their way.

Katie's party went on, it was much better now.

How come? They were using MANNERS, that's how.

Do you have these books by Scott E. Sutton?

The Kuekumber Kids™ Series

The Kuekumber Kids Meet The Alphabet Alien
The Kuekumber Kids Meet The Numberasaurus
The Kuekumber Kids Meet The Sheik of Shapes
The Kuekumber Kids Meet The Professor of Paint
The Kuekumber Kids Meet The Monster of Manners

The Family of Ree™ Adventures

The Family of Ree
Oh, No, More Wizard Lessons!
The Secret of Gorbee Grotto
More Altitude, Quick!
Look at the Size of That Long-Legged Ploot!
The Legend of the Snow Pookas

The Adventures of Dinosaur Dog™

#1, Tyrannosaurus Forrest
#2, Danger: Dinky Diplodocus
#3, The Trouble With Pteranodons

For free information on these and other books visit our web site at
http://www.actionpublishing.com or write to us at the address below.
To locate the closest store carrying books by Scott E. Sutton call
(800) 644-2665.

ACTION
PUBLISHING

PO Box 391, Glendale CA 91209